In Ms. Kimball's class we get to do lots of

neat things.

Last week we walked to the park near school.

We had a picnic and played on the swings.

And Ms. Kimball even went down the slide

with us!

Today Ms. Kimball brought two rabbits to school.

Everybody will take turns feeding them.

Peter and I got to feed them first.

We cleaned out their cage, too.

Rabbits are messy.

Ms. Kimball said, "Danny, you and Peter

did a good job."

After story time Ms. Kimball says, "I won't

be at school tomorrow.

I have to go away for a while.

My mother has been sick and she needs my help.

You'll have another teacher until I come back."

We all have new jobs to do while

Ms. Kimball's gone.

When we get to school, a tall man is at the

door to our room.

"Hi kids!" he says.

"I'm Mr. Coleman. I'll be your teacher

until Ms. Kimball comes back.

What are your names?"

I don't want to tell him my name.

Everything in the room looks different.

All the games and books are put away.

I don't think I'm going to like

this teacher.

Peter and I want to play with our fort.

But the blocks are back on the shelves.

We have to start all over again.

Peter gets mad.

I tell him, "I bet *he* put them away!"

When it's time to clean up, Mr. Coleman says,

"Sarah and Peter can be in charge of the paints."

"That's not fair!" I shout. "Ms. Kimball said

Peter and I could do it, not Sarah!"

I push Sarah away.

The paint can falls on the table and spills.

Mr. Coleman helps me clean up the paint.

He says, "I didn't know you two boys were in charge of the paints.

I bet you feel mad at me."

I say, "Yeah. I wish Ms. Kimball was here.

She always lets us do stuff together."

I stop at Peter's house and we walk

to school together.

Peter says, "I hope Ms. Kimball's back today."

He kicks a stone in the street.

I say, "Me too. I don't like this teacher.

Sometimes I hate school."

We're going to make cranberry sauce today.

Mr. Coleman puts the grinder together.

It's fun to grind up the berries with oranges
and nuts.

The cranberry sauce tastes really good!

At recess, Mr. Coleman plays jump rope

with us.

He's fun!

When we choose up sides for tag, Peter says,

"We want Mr. Coleman!"

Mr. Coleman shows us how to join hands

for a circle dance.

We stamp our feet in time to the music.

I get dizzy when we go around too fast!

Sometimes we get all mixed up and start to laugh.

After school, Mr. Coleman talks to Peter and me.

"I know you must miss your teacher.

I'm sure she misses you, too.

But until she gets back, will you boys help me?

I don't know where some things are kept."

Peter and I tell him, "Sure, we'll help!"

Ms. Kimball is back today!

She asks us what we did while she was gone.

"We made cranberry sauce and learned a dance,"

we tell her.

"And Mr. Coleman played jump rope, too!"

Ms. Kimball says, "It sounds like you had fun

with Mr. Coleman."

Peter and I look at each other. I guess we're

going to miss Mr. Coleman, too.

Design   Interface Design Group